A POCKET FOR CORDUROY

A POCKET FOR CORDUROY

story and pictures by DON FREEMAN

Puffin Books

To Takako Nishinoya,

who knows how a bear feels about pockets

A bear's share of the author's royalties from the sale of *A Pocket For Corduroy* goes to the *Don and Lydia Freeman Research Fund* to support psychological research concerning children afflicted with cancer.

PUFFIN BOOKS
Published by the Penguin Group
Penguin Putnam Books for Young Readers, 345 Hudson Street, New York, New York 10014, U.S.A.
Penguin Books Ltd, 27 Wrights Lane, London W8 5TZ, England
Penguin Books Australia Ltd, Ringwood, Victoria, Australia
Penguin Books Canada Ltd, 10 Alcorn Avenue, Toronto, Ontario, Canada M4V 3B2
Penguin Books (N.Z.) Ltd, 182-190 Wairau Road, Auckland 10, New Zealand
Penguin Books Ltd, Registered Offices: Harmondsworth, Middlesex, England

First published by The Viking Press 1978
Published in Picture Puffins 1980
66 67 68 69 70

Library of Congress Cataloging in Publication Data
Freeman, Don. A pocket for Corduroy.
Summary: A toy bear who wants a pocket for
himself searches for one in a laundromat.
(1. Toys-Fiction   2. Pockets-Fiction)
I. Title.   PZ8.9.F85Po   (E)   79-92744   ISBN 978-0-14-050352-4

Manufactured in China

Late one summer afternoon Lisa and her mother took their laundry to the laundromat.

As always on such trips Lisa carried along her toy bear, Corduroy.

The laundromat was a very busy place at this hour.

"Now, Corduroy, you sit right here and wait for me," Lisa said. "I'm going to help with our wash."

Corduroy waited patiently. Then he suddenly perked up his ears.

Lisa's mother was saying, "Be sure to take everything out of your pockets, Lisa dear. You don't want your precious things to get all wet and soapy."

"Pockets?" said Corduroy to himself. "I don't have a pocket!"

He slid off the chair. "I must go find something to make a pocket out of," he said, and he began to look around.

First he came to a pile of fancy towels and washcloths, but nothing was the right size or color.

Then he saw a huge stack of colorful clothes in a laundry bag. "There ought to be something in there to make a pocket out of," he said.

Without hesitating, he climbed inside the bag, which was filled with pieces of wet laundry. The dampness didn't bother Corduroy in the least. "This must be a cave," he said, sighing happily. "I've always wanted to live in a dark, cool cave."

When the time came for Lisa to fetch her bear, he was gone.

"Oh, Mommy!" she exclaimed. "Corduroy isn't here where I left him!"

"I'm sorry, honey," said her mother, "but the laundromat will be closing soon and we must be getting home."

Lisa was reluctant to leave without Corduroy, but her mother insisted.
"You can come back tomorrow," she said. "I'm sure he will still be here."

As they left, a young man wearing an artist's beret was taking his wet laundry out of a bag—the very bag Corduroy had discovered!

Before he knew it, Corduroy was being tossed, together with all the sheets, shirts, shorts, and slacks . . .

inside the dryer.

But just as the artist was shutting the glass door, Corduroy tumbled out onto the floor.

"How in thunder did that bear ever get mixed up with all my things?" the artist wondered.

Poor Corduroy was damp all over.

"The least I can do for him is give his overalls a good drying," said the man thoughtfully. He unbuttoned Corduroy's shoulder straps and put his overalls in the dryer.

Corduroy grew dizzy as he watched the clothes spinning around, but the artist became inspired. "This would make a wonderful painting!" he said as he took a sketch pad out of his pocket and began drawing the swirling colors. "I can hardly wait to get back to my studio."

Finally the dryer stopped whirling and the man gathered up the clothes. Then he helped Corduroy put on his warm, dry overalls.

All at once the manager of the laundromat called, "Closing time! Everybody out!"

Corduroy was gently placed on top of a washing machine.

"I wonder who that bear belongs to," said the artist as he was leaving.
"Seems to me he should have his name someplace. He's too fine a fellow
to be lost."

As soon as the lights were turned off, Corduroy began his search again. He was surprised to see something white glowing in the dark. "Maybe it's snow!" he said excitedly. "I've always wanted to play in the snow."

He accidentally tipped over the open-lidded box, and suddenly he
was covered with soft, slippery soap flakes.
Gradually Corduroy began to slip and slide....

"Oh, what fun!" he said with a smile. "I've always wanted to ski down
a steep mountainside."

He landed paws first in an empty laundry basket.

"This must be a cage," he said, peeking through the bars. "I've *never* wanted to live inside a cage like a bear in the zoo!"

But by now Corduroy felt drowsy, and soon he nodded off to sleep.

Next morning when the manager came to open the door of the laundromat, there was Lisa waiting.

"I left something here yesterday," she explained. "May I look around?"

"Certainly," said the manager. "My customers are always leaving things."

Lisa was searching under the chairs and in back of the washing machines when she heard the manager call her. "Is this what you're looking for, señorita?"

"Yes, yes! He's my best friend!" shouted Lisa as she came running.
She reached in and picked Corduroy out of the basket. "So this is where
you've been, you little rascal!" she said. "It's time I took you home!"

Lisa thanked the manager and ran out the door and down the street, holding Corduroy tightly in her arms. "I thought I told you to wait for me," she said. "Why did you wander away?"

"I went looking for a pocket," Corduroy said.

"Oh, Corduroy! Why didn't you tell me you wanted a pocket?" asked Lisa, giving him an affectionate squeeze.

That very morning Lisa sewed a pocket on Corduroy's overalls.
"And here is a card I've made with your name on it for you to keep
tucked inside," she said.

"I've always wanted a purple pocket with my name tucked inside,"
said Corduroy as he and Lisa nuzzled noses.